THE Spectacular CITY

Teresa Heapy • David Litchfield

Mouse and Bear lived in a little,
dark house in the big, black Woods.

Mouse made inventions
and Bear made tea,
and today Mouse wanted to go to
the Spectacular City.

"Bear," said Mouse, "just look at those lights!
They twinkle SO bright and SO fast and SO clear.
Let's leave our dark Woods and go to the City
and live in that sparkle and glitter and shine!"

"OK, Mouse, if you want to," said Bear with a smile.
"Just let me fold this paper and then –"

"There's no time, Bear," said Mouse. "Let's go!"

So Mouse and
Bear went . . .

. . . to the shimmering City.
There were dazzling lights
stretching up to the sky.
"Look up, Bear," said Mouse.
"WOW!"

"It's so busy," said Bear. "Mouse, remember –
I've got you and you've got me.
So if we lose each other, just call, and I'll come."
"Yes, yes, Bear," said Mouse.
"Now, where to first?"

"Can I help you?" a voice murmured out from an alley.
Mouse spun round. "Who's there?"

"I'm Cat," said the voice, slipping out of the velvet.
"I help new folks around – I can show you the way."

"Yes, please!" breathed Mouse.
"Where's the brightest, shiniest place that you know?"

"Ah, my friend," said Cat,
"let me show you . . .

the City!"

So Cat led
the way,

and Mouse
and Bear
followed

all over the
beaming,
bright,
bustling
City . . .

through
neon-lit
alleys

and
kaleidoscope
streets.

But still Mouse
wanted more.
"More
light!
More
light!"

Cat said, "Then,
my friend,
come with me
to the Glitz!"

She waved her paw at a glittering restaurant,
perched high on top of a skyscraper point.

At the door was a sign.

"Oh dear," said Mouse. "Bear – you don't mind?"
"Er . . . no. You go," said Bear.
"But remember – just call, and I'll come."

And Bear went, looking back,
as Mouse strode off with Cat.

Mouse and Cat sat in the skyscraper restaurant,
looking out on a glistening river of light.

"I'll have the Cheese Special," said Mouse.
"And, Cat, what will *you* eat?"

"Well, of course," said Cat, "*I'll* eat . . .

YOU!

With a dash of paprika and pepper and salt!"
Her green eyes gleamed as she crept towards Mouse.

"N-no, you won't!" stammered Mouse.
It was time to call . . .

"BEAR!"

WANTED

"MOUSE!
I'm coming!"
called Bear,

and he rushed
to the rescue
with a bundle
of paper,

folding
corners
and
creases

as he
hurried
along.

"On the roof!"
shouted Mouse.

"ON THE
ROOF!"

Mouse was trapped in a skyscraper corner.
"You can't eat me – I'm your new friend!"
"Just one step," muttered Cat,
"and, my friend,
you'll be SUPPER."

She stalked one paw,
then two . . .

when in flew . . .

BEAR!

Bear swooped by in a plane made of paper – the most perfect, particular, powerful plane.

Glitz Glitz Glit

"Come on, Mouse! Get in!"
shouted Bear, as Cat sprang,
her fur flying.

"So long, Cat," said Bear.

"Bear, I'm sorry," said Mouse,
"and thank you for . . . everything.
Let's say goodbye to those twinkling lights."

Bear said, "But, Mouse . . .

. . . just look at the stars!
Remember, I've got you, and you've got me,
and we've got all the light now
that we'll ever need."

And Mouse and Bear flew in the plane made of paper,
on through the glowing Milky Way foam.

On through the sparkle, the gleam and the glitter,
as stars whispered lullabies
and showed the way home.

The End

How To MAKE

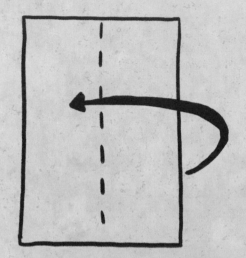

1. Fold the paper in half, vertically.

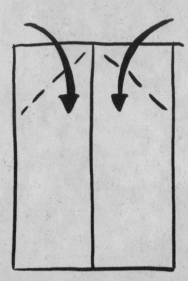

2. Unfold the paper and fold each of the top corners into the centre line.

3. Now fold the top edges into the centre line.

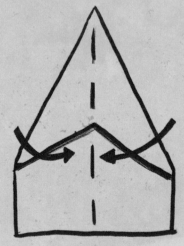

4. Fold the plane in half towards you.

A Paper Plane
(DRAWN BY BEAR)

5.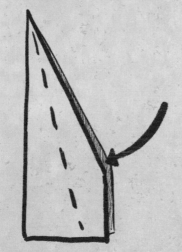

Fold the wings down,
matching the top edges
with the bottom edge
of the body.

6.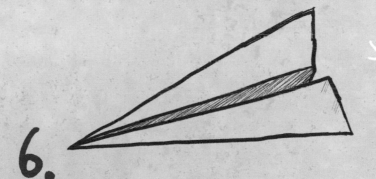

Fly your plane!

FINISHED

For Enzo – T.H.
For Katie, Ben & George – D.L.

RED FOX

UK | USA | Canada | Ireland | Australia | India | New Zealand | South Africa

Red Fox is part of the Penguin Random House group of companies
whose addresses can be found at global.penguinrandomhouse.com.

www.penguin.co.uk   www.puffin.co.uk   www.ladybird.co.uk

Penguin
Random House
UK

First published 2018
001

Printed in China
A CIP catalogue record for this book is available from the British Library

ISBN: 978–1–782–95676–1

All correspondence to:
Red Fox, Penguin Random House Children's
80 Strand, London WC2R 0RL

FSC
www.fsc.org
MIX
Paper from
responsible sources
FSC® C018179

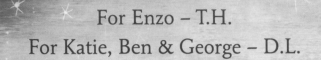